Whale Music

by Becky Cheston
illustrated by Karen Jerome

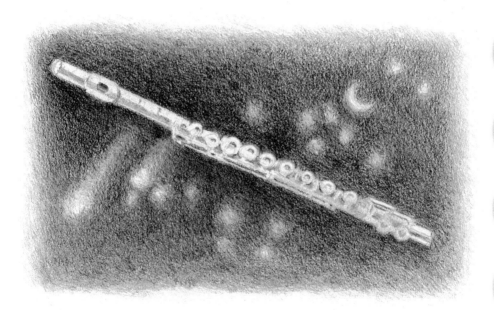

HOUGHTON MIFFLIN   BOSTON

I know this beach as well as anyone even though I can't see it. I know the sound of surf on the shore, and the smell of seaweed drying in the sun. I know that the music I play on my flute floats gently out to the horizon on the offshore breezes.

My father is captain of *The Krill*, a whale-watch boat. Today, something seems wrong. I can tell by the change in my father's voice at breakfast.

Someone stomps up our porch. "Clara, are your folks in?" It's Brian, from the Ocean Institute. "There's a whale stranded on the beach—a young humpback."

My stomach tumbles. Last year another whale had stranded itself on the beach. It never made it back to the water. I know that unless Brian can get this humpback out to sea, it will die too.

"What happened?" I ask.

"We don't know," Brian says. "We'll need special equipment to rescue it, though. In the meantime, we need to keep it from drying out. I'm organizing a bucket brigade."

Ruthie takes Gregory and me to the quay. Our ticket booth is busy with people curious about why the tours are cancelled today. Other people ask what's happening at the beach. Gregory looks through his binoculars and reports.

"Lots of people are standing around," he says. "I can see Mommy and Daddy! They're giving the whale a bath!"

"Actually, they're pouring water on the whale to keep it wet," says Ruthie. "If it dries out, it will be in big trouble."

At the wharf I talk to Barney, one of the fishermen. "Why don't they just push the whale back into the ocean?" I ask.

"It's too big for that," Barney says. "The Institute has a special team coming from Nova Scotia to tug the whale out to sea. Until they get here, Brian and the folks have to keep it wet."

But by nightfall, the Canadian team has not arrived. As Ruthie sets out our dinner, Mom makes sandwiches for the bucket brigade.

"Thank goodness for all the volunteers," says Mom.

I sit on the porch, playing my music. I think about the whale as I play. I imagine the music floating on the breeze down to the beach. I imagine that the whale can hear it.

I hear my parents climbing the stairs. Their footsteps are slow and heavy.

"What's going on?" I ask.

"The team from Nova Scotia still isn't here," says Dad. "The longer the whale is out of the ocean, the harder it will be to save him."

"Poor thing," I say. "It must be terrified."

"You're right about that," says Mom. "But Dad and I have an idea."

Dad and I walk down to the beach together. I've known the way for as long as I can remember. The feel of the wooden slats of the walkway under my feet and the smell of the water guide me. As we walk, Dad quietly tells me his plan.

At the beach, I hear people talking. They're still wetting down the whale. I can sense the animal just a few yards away. I can hear its breathing. Dad leads me to the water's edge. We walk very slowly and carefully.

I let go of Dad's hand for a second and walk a little closer towards the whale.

"Careful," says Dad. "Not too close."

Dad grabs my hand again. I know not to get much closer. Suddenly, I can feel just how scared the animal must be. I stand still and quiet.

"You're afraid," I say to the whale in a low voice.

"Okay, kid," says Dad. "Do your thing."

I step back on the dry sand and put the flute to my lips. I try to seesaw the sounds in long whale-like tones.

"Keep playing, Sugar," whispers Dad. "I think he likes it."

I play on and on. I lose sense of how long I've been here. I lose sense of anyone else on the beach. It's just the whale, the music, and me.

"Hey, Stan. Clara. Will you look at that!" a familiar voice cries out. It's Brian. He's come with a group of people whose voices I don't know.

"I've been playing music for the whale," I say.

"We can see that," says a woman. "There's nothing better for a scared humpback than a little whale music."

I sit in the sand and keep playing as Dad, Brian, and the Canadians make plans for the rescue. They'll start at first light.

I'll be there too, sending the giant animal safely on its way to the sounds of whale music.

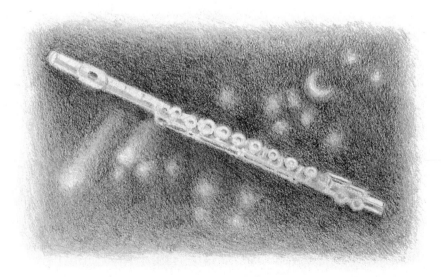